Mr. Football Bakes a Pie

by Lisa Klobuchar

Printed in the United States of America

ISBN 0-15-313956-0

Ordering Options
ISBN 0-15-314006-2 (Grade 6 Collection)
ISBN 0-15-314162-X (package of 5)

1 2 3 4 5 6 7 8 9 10 026 99 98

Anton was the best football player at Jackson Middle School, but he couldn't cook. Although this problem may not seem serious, Anton's Home Ec mishaps were about to earn him his first failing grade. That grade would mean he'd have to sit out the big game against Jackson's rivals, the Wallace Bulldogs.

On Monday, less than two weeks before the big game, Ms. Sorgenson announced that the final Home Ec project was to bake an apple pie.

"Here is a sign-up sheet," said Ms. Sorgenson. "By Friday, give me your order for all the ingredients you'll need. The school will buy them for you. You'll be baking a week from today."

"All I know about apples is that Mr. Lewis guards the ones on his tree as if they're made of gold," Anton said to Eric. "I know even less about baking an apple pie. I'm a dead man."

"No problem," said Eric. "I'll teach you how to make a pie."

Anton patched together his first crust as well as he could. However, after the pie was baked, it looked as if it had been in an accident. It tasted even worse.

In the meantime, Anton's football practices were disasters. He missed easy passes. When he kicked the ball, it ricocheted off the scoreboard. His coach said, "What's your problem?" Anton couldn't tell him the truth—he could think of nothing but that apple pie.

Day after day, Anton kept baking, and with Eric's help, each pie was better than the last. Finally, Anton's seventh pie was a winner.

On Monday morning Anton felt good. His apple filling was sweet and rich. His crust was golden and flaky. While he and Eric walked to school, Anton looked over his recipe. Eric asked him, "So what kind of apples did you order?"

Anton stopped in his tracks. "Oh no!"

"You forgot to order the ingredients?" Eric asked. "Class starts in forty minutes!"

Anton galloped the nine blocks back to his house in record time. He burst into the kitchen and got flour, salt, cinnamon, sugar, and butter. But to his horror, there were no apples. Where could he get apples? The nearest store was five blocks in the opposite direction, and Anton had no money.

"I'm doomed! No pie, no football," Anton whined. "It doesn't matter," he sighed. "My football playing stinks anyway." Then he remembered Mr. Lewis's tree.

He rang his neighbor's doorbell. The old man opened the door. "What do you want?" Mr. Lewis asked in an abrupt tone.

"Mr. Lewis," Anton said, "I'm baking a pie for school today, and we're out of apples. Could I take a few from your tree?"

"If you can find any," said Mr. Lewis with a chuckle.

The branches were bare except for six large, rosy apples. They were poised at the end of a limb high above. Anton had an idea. He retrieved his football from his backyard and ran back to the tree. He took aim, breathed deeply, and threw. The ball sailed straight through the branches and struck the apples. They quivered, and then tumbled to his feet.

Anton ran back to school. He slipped into the Home Ec room just as the bell rang. "Ahh, I see Anton has decided to cook with us today after all," said Ms. Sorgenson. Still winded, Anton smiled and got to work.

The next day, Ms. Sorgenson said Anton's pie was one of the best she'd ever tasted. On Friday, Anton led the Jackson Mustangs to a sixteen-point victory. When Eric asked Anton how it felt, he answered, "Almost as sweet as apple pie."

A Football Hero

Create a football card for Anton. Make up any information you don't know.

George Smith	
School Team	Galileo Broncos
Height	5'9"
Weight	145
Born	June 4, 1984
Position	Fullback
Fumbles	3
Points Scored	0
Other Interests	

Anton	
School	
Height	
Weight	
Born	
Position	
Fumbles	
Points Scored	
Other Interests	